baseball

Other Books in the Sports Heroes Series

baseball

Mark Littleton

Zonderkidz

Zonder**kidz**™

The children's group of Zondervan

www.zonderkidz.com

Sports Heroes: Baseball
Copyright © 2002 by Mark Littleton

Requests for information should be addressed to:
Grand Rapids, Michigan 49530

ISBN: 0–310–70291–7

Editor: Barbara Scott
Art direction: Lisa Workman
Cover design: Alan Close
Cover photography: Jeff Gross / Allsport
Interior design: Todd Sprague
Interior photography: Allsport

Printed in the United States of America

02 03 04 05 06 07 /❖DC/ 10 9 8 7 6 5 4 3 2 1

ACKNOWLEDGMENTS

Thanks to my editor Barbara Scott for her diligence; Zonderkidz publisher Gary Richardson for hanging in there with me; and my wife Jeanette for spending my advance check on cool stuff I really love.

*To my Uncle Harry (deceased) and Aunt Beth,
who always made me feel loved and at home in
their home.*

CONTENTS

1

JOHN OLERUD:
Hitting Steady, Hitting Hard

Personal	Height: 6′ 5″ Weight: 220
	Spouse: Kelly
	Kids: Garrett John
	Birth date: August 5, 1968, Seattle,
	    Washington
	Schools: Interlake High School,
	    Bellevue, Washington
	    Washington State University

Professional	Team: Seattle Mariners Throws: Left Bats: Left Position: First Base

Records and Stats	AL single-season record for most inten-
	    tional bases on balls: 33 (1993)
	In 1998, set NL single-season record for
	    most consecutive times reached base
	    safely: 15 (September 16 [1], 18 [5],
	    20 [4], 22 [1]—6 singles, 1 double, 2
	    home runs, and 6 bases on balls).
	Tied for AL lead with 10 sacrifice flies
	    in 1991
	26-game hitting streak (May 26-June 22,
	    1993)
	.473 on-base percentage in 1993
	AL batting title, 1993.
	23-game hitting streak (July 19-August
	    9, 1998)
	Starter on 2001 All-Star Team
	One of two players to hit for the cycle
	    in both leagues

Photo by: Otto Greule Jr. / Allsport

Career Batting Stats

YEAR	TM	G	AB	R	H	2B	3B	HR	RBI	BB	IBB	K	SB	CS	OBP	SLG	AVG
1989	Tor	6	8	2	3	0	0	0	0	0	0	1	0	0	.375	.375	.375
1990	Tor	111	358	43	95	15	1	14	48	57	6	75	0	2	.364	.430	.265
1991	Tor	139	454	64	116	30	1	17	68	68	9	84	0	2	.353	.438	.256
1992	Tor	138	458	68	130	28	0	16	66	70	11	61	1	0	.375	.450	.284
1993	Tor	158	551	109	200	54	2	24	107	114	33	65	0	2	.473	.599	.363
1994	Tor	108	384	47	114	29	2	12	67	61	12	53	1	2	.393	.477	.297
1995	Tor	135	492	72	143	32	0	8	54	84	10	54	0	0	.398	.404	.291
1996	Tor	125	398	59	109	25	0	18	61	60	6	37	1	0	.382	.472	.274
1997	NYM	154	524	90	154	34	1	22	102	85	5	67	0	0	.400	.489	.294
1998	NYM	160	557	91	197	36	4	22	93	96	11	73	2	2	.447	.551	.354
1999	NYM	162	581	107	173	39	0	19	96	125	5	66	3	0	.427	.463	.298
2000	Sea	159	565	84	161	45	0	14	103	102	11	96	0	2	.392	.439	.285
2001	Sea	159	572	91	173	32	1	21	95	94	9	70	3	1	.401	.472	.302
TOTALS		1714	5902	927	1768	399	12	207	960	1016	128	802	11	13	.404	.476	.300

Not many first basemen win batting titles. But few who saw John Olerud play during his high school and college years were surprised when John won the American League batting title in 1993. He won it with a .363 average; through early August, he was hitting .400. He also logged 54 doubles, 24 home runs, and 107 RBIs. He definitely made a big contribution to the Toronto Blue Jays winning the World Series that year.

A reporter asked him some years later, "Do you think you can hit .363 again?"

John, always cautious and soft-spoken, said, "It [1993] was a very good year for me. Everything went right. I just felt awfully good at the plate. I swung the bat real well. I had good plate coverage and good balance. Do I think I can do it again? Yes, I think

I'm capable of hitting at that level. The last couple of years, I've gotten some bad mechanics in my swing. I haven't felt that same feeling as ninety-three.... [I must] go back to the basics and try to get that same rhythm, timing, and balance back. That's what I'm working on."

John's dedication to improving his game has made him a crowd favorite. Fans see him as the consistent, reliable lefty. He rarely makes errors at first base, and, with a bat in his hand, he is always a hard out. He knows how to read a pitcher.

In 1993, John made a serious run at the incredible .400 average mark, last achieved by Ted Williams in 1941, with a .406 average. On June 28, 1993, John was hitting .401 and enjoying a 25-game hitting streak. Before 1993, the last major-league player to hit over .400 that late in the season was George Brett in 1980. (Brett made it to August hitting over .400. But he ended up the season with a .390 average.)

Baseball Quiz

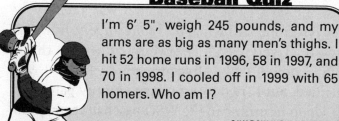

I'm 6' 5", weigh 245 pounds, and my arms are as big as many men's thighs. I hit 52 home runs in 1996, 58 in 1997, and 70 in 1998. I cooled off in 1999 with 65 homers. Who am I?

Answer: Mark McGwire

John finished a bit below Williams's mark but well enough to win the batting title. Being the best hitter in the big leagues is no small achievement. And it almost never happened. In fact, he is blessed to be playing baseball at all.

Early in his career, on January 11, 1989, John collapsed in the field house at Washington State University while playing on the college baseball team. He'd put in an early-morning workout and noticed something was wrong. Moments later, he fell to the ground, nearly comatose. An ambulance sped him to the hospital.

What had happened? John's brain was bleeding into his spinal column. He languished in a hospital bed until six weeks later, when doctors removed an aneurysm from the bottom of his brain. He returned home from the hospital, and six weeks later he went back to play for Washington State.

John won't forget that moment when he was wheeled into the operating room.

"I remember how scary it was, how weird it was," he says. "The doctors said it was a relatively easy operation, but when it's brain surgery, how can it be relatively easy? The weird thing was that I didn't know if I'd be alive afterwards. Inside I was petrified, but I tried to act relaxed for my parents."

Upon returning to the WSU baseball team, John hit .359 with 30 RBIs, in only 27 games. Three months later, the Toronto Blue Jays called him directly on to their squad, making him only the sixteenth player in history to skip the minor-league system.

Toronto craved John's talents, especially as a hitter. When it comes to batting, John Olerud is said to have a dream swing. Few players achieve it. But he connects with the ball easily and consistently.

With his prowess at the plate, John developed into a leading contender for the batting title. He recalls that during spring training one year, Paul Molitor and he were dressing before a game. Molitor, who hadn't said but "hi" and "how're ya doin'" to John all season, suddenly asked, "When are you going to win a batting title?"

"What do you mean?" John answered.

"You've got the best swing, and you hit the ball more consistent than anyone I've ever seen."

At that moment, for the first time in his life, John believed he *could* win the batting crown. Six months later, he did. His confidence in himself and his abilities paid off on the field. In life, John displays an even greater faith—his faith in God.

For many years, John has been a man of faith, a family man whose beliefs have sustained him through tough times as well as good times. He married Kelly Plaisted before he ever got into the majors. His son, Garrett, was born three years ago.

Garrett's birth was an awesome moment for John, as a father and a man of God. Even more than the batting title, this little creation of God was his.

"The big thing that God's shown me in Garrett's birth is how much He loves me," John says. "You really get a feel for what it's like to be a part of creation. In a way, he's our creation. In a way, he is made in our image. The unconditional love we have for him helps show God's unconditional love for us."

John is not known for being talkative or for his sense of humor, but he perks up when necessary. "I like humor, and I like to laugh," he says. His favorite Stooge of the Three Stooges is Curly because John thinks he is the funniest. His contract with the Mariners is nothing to laugh about, though. He

OCTOBER

8

1956

A Great Day in Baseball

Don Larsen of the New York Yankees retires all 27 batters in the World Series, pitching a perfect game.

recently inked a three-year, $20-million deal that is up for renegotiation before the 2002 season.

Part of the reason he's paid so well goes back to the fact that he is a .301 lifetime hitter and an all-around team player. Anyone who keeps up with baseball will spot John's name in the leader's stats in the sports section of the newspaper. John often makes the list for total hits and batting average.

Baseball, though, sometimes pushes one to make hard choices. John's transition to Seattle wasn't easy. He left the Mets when they were on a World Series course in 1999, although they didn't make it that far. Even though he grew up in Seattle, he says, "It's hard to leave a good situation and go to an unknown situation. You would think going

Baseball Humor

When the baseball players staged their ill-fated strike in 1994 and almost lost the fans' love and affection, many of the replacement players the league was using to break the strike weren't exactly in top shape. During a Pittsburgh-Minnesota game, an angry fan yelled at a rather heavy, unshaven, out-of-shape man, "Look at you—you're a disgrace. You're not a player!"

And in reality, he wasn't. That player was Pirate coach Tommy Sandt.

JUNE
12
1974

A Great Day in Baseball

Little League baseball announced on this day that girls could play in the league, along with the boys. On August 23, 1989, Victoria Bruckner played in the Little League World Series and scored three runs for her team from San Pedro, California.

back home would be a good situation, but there were a lot of unknowns. I didn't know a whole lot about the coaching staff or the guys on the team."

Nonetheless, John quickly made connections in Seattle. Catcher Dan Wilson, also a Christian, and backup catcher Tom Lampkin invited John to their Bible studies on the road. This helped John fit in much more quickly. He felt welcomed and accepted.

John has made his mark on Seattle because of those friendships, as well as his play on the field. He's a quiet sort of guy, one who lets his skills do his talking. He's reserved in social settings and media interviews. But he's happy to step up to the plate and rock the world. As Seattle manager Lou Piniella says, "Just let him play. Let his bat and glove do the talking."

Mini-Moment of Truth in Baseball History with Joe Carter

The World Series, 1993. Game 6. The Toronto Blue Jays lead the Philadelphia Phillies, 3 games to 2. And the Phillies lead this game 6–5 in the ninth inning. Mitch Williams, the Phillies' ace closer, is pitching against Joe Carter. Williams can be wild, but he has saved 43 games in 51 attempts during the season. There are two men on base, Rickey Henderson on a walk, and Paul Molitor via a single. The count goes to 2 and 1, and then Williams throws a slider. Carter swings and misses.

With the count at two balls and two strikes, catcher Darren Daulton calls for another slider. The philosophy — if it works, keep using it.

But Williams shakes off his catcher's signal. He wants to bring the heat, the fastball. Daulton gives in. OK, he signals, serve up a fastball.

Williams winds up. The pitch comes in. Carter likes the look of it, but he knows he often hooks these pitches foul. Still, he swings.

Wham! The ball is in the air. Carter loses it in the lights. He's on the way to first base.

He sees the ball again as he reaches first. It's over the fence. Home run. Three runs score, and it's 8–6, Blue Jays. The Series is over; Toronto has taken the title for the second year in a row.

And Joe Carter has done what every kid and baseball lover has dreamed about: hit a game-winning home run in the ninth in the last game of the Series.

Suddenly, Joe Carter is a hero like he's never been before.

2

JOHN SMOLTZ:
Pitching Them Hard and on Target

Personal	Height: 6′ 3″ Weight: 220
	Spouse: Dyan Kids: John Andrew Jr.,
	    Rachel Elizabeth, and Carly Maria
	Hometown: Duluth, Georgia
	Birth date: May 15, 1967, in Warren,
	    Michigan
	Schools: Waverly High School, Lansing,
	    Michigan

Professional	Team: Atlanta Braves Bats: Right Throws: Right Position: Pitcher

Records and Stats	NL Cy Young Award in 1996.
	Led majors in wins, strikeouts, and
	    strikeouts per nine innings (9.8).
	Led NL in innings pitched and win-
	    ning percentage .750 (24–8).
	Played in fourth All-Star game of his
	    career; earned start and win.
	1995: Second in the NL with 193
	    strikeouts.
	1993: Won 15 games. Second consecu-
	    tive All-Star team, third overall.
	    New NLCS record with 44 career
	    strikeouts
	1992: Named MVP of the 1992 NLCS.
	    Led NL pitchers with 215 strike-
	    outs. 15 wins and three shutouts

Career Pitching Stats

YEAR	TM	G	GS	CG	SHO	IP	H	R	ER	HR	BB	K	W	L	SV	WHIP	ERA
1988	Atl	12	12	0	0	64.0	74	40	39	10	33	37	2	7	0	1.67	5.48
1989	Atl	29	29	5	0	208.0	160	79	68	15	72	168	12	11	0	1.12	2.94
1990	Atl	34	34	6	2	231.1	206	109	99	20	90	170	14	11	0	1.28	3.85
1991	Atl	36	36	5	0	229.2	206	101	97	16	77	148	14	13	0	1.23	3.80
1992	Atl	35	35	9	3	246.2	206	90	78	17	80	215	15	12	0	1.16	2.85
1993	Atl	35	35	3	1	243.2	208	104	98	23	100	208	15	11	0	1.26	3.62
1994	Atl	21	21	1	0	134.2	120	69	62	15	48	113	6	10	0	1.25	4.14
1995	Atl	29	29	2	1	192.2	166	76	68	15	72	193	12	7	0	1.24	3.18
1996	Atl	35	35	6	2	253.2	199	93	83	19	55	276	24	8	0	1.00	2.94
1997	Atl	35	35	7	2	256.0	234	97	86	21	63	241	15	12	0	1.16	3.02
1998	Atl	26	26	2	2	167.2	145	58	54	10	44	173	17	3	0	1.13	2.90
1999	Atl	29	29	1	1	186.1	168	70	66	14	40	156	11	8	0	1.12	3.19
2001	Atl	36	5	0	0	59.0	53	24	22	7	10	57	3	3	10	1.67	3.36
TOTALS		392	361	47	14	2473.1	2145	1010	920	202	784	2155	160	116	10	1.19	3.35

World Series Record

YEAR	CLUB	W-L	ERA	G	GS	CG	SHO	SV	IP	H	R	ER	BB	SO
1991	Atl vs. Min	0–0	1.26	2	2	0	0	0	14.1	13	2	2	1	11
1992	Atl vs. Tor	1–0	2.70	2	2	0	0	0	13.1	13	5	4	7	12
1995	Atl vs. Cle	0–0	15.43	1	1	0	0	0	2.1	6	4	4	2	4
1996	Atl vs. NYY	1–1	0.64	2	2	0	0	0	14.0	6	2	1	8	14
TOTALS		2–1	2.25	7	7	0	0	0	44.0	38	13	11	18	41

John Smoltz, pitcher extraordinaire, Cy Young winner, and strikeout king, loves to play basketball.

Yes, basketball was his first sports passion. He was All-State in baseball and basketball at his high school in Michigan. And he loved putting the ball through the hoop.

But he was better at putting a much smaller ball across a plate.

So, that settled it. John Smoltz would pursue a career in baseball.

Anyone who has batted against John knows he's up against a force of nature. John's fastball sizzles across the plate at speeds of 90 mph plus. He has a great curve and a battery of other pitches, including a changeup and a knuckleball. John stands on the mound, fearless and concentrating. When he goes into his stretch, he studies runners, looks at the plate, and then nails it: Strike one!

John doesn't often get behind in the count. He likes to throw hard, harder, and hardest. In 2000, though, he underwent Tommy John surgery on his elbow (Tommy John, a former pitcher for several teams, made a great comeback after having this surgery). Many wondered if Smoltz would throw again. He sat out most of the 2000 season.

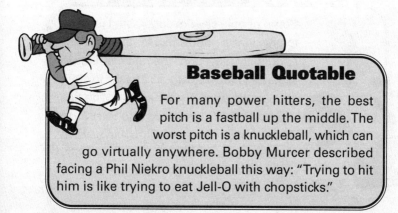

Baseball Quotable

For many power hitters, the best pitch is a fastball up the middle. The worst pitch is a knuckleball, which can go virtually anywhere. Bobby Murcer described facing a Phil Niekro knuckleball this way: "Trying to hit him is like trying to eat Jell-O with chopsticks."

The injury threatened to shorten a brilliant career. Shortly before winning the Cy Young Award in 1996, John became the Braves' first 20-game winner since 1993. He ended up breaking Phil Niekro's 1969 Atlanta record with 24 wins.

Scouts and baseball commentators began to realize his potential after he was traded by the Detroit Tigers to Atlanta in 1987 for veteran pitcher Doyle Alexander. John put in a couple of years in Atlanta's minor-league system, then burst into the show in 1989, ultimately making it to the All-Star Game.

For much of his career with the Braves, John has been part of a rotation that includes pitchers like Greg Maddux and Tom Glavine—elite talent to play with. Yet, John has made his own mark, appearing in the All-Star Game four times and mak-

Baseball Quiz

Some people say I'm cocky, but I just like to give fans a good show for their money. I originally played for the Yankees. I hit 14 triples in 1992 and stole 56 bases in 1997, and I'm the only guy in baseball who has played in the Super Bowl and the World Series. I also became a Christian several years ago, and my life has radically changed. Do you know who I am?

Answer: Deion Sanders

ing it into four World Series. He has a career 2.25 ERA in seven World Series games. In 1996, he gave up only one earned run in 14 innings against the Yankees.

Still, with all the acclaim, John remains a relatively quiet guy who loves to tell lousy jokes and play a bit of Nintendo. In fact, Jeff Foxworthy, of "You might be a redneck, if ..." fame, once invited John to his house to play Nintendo Baseball All-Stars.

"The doorbell rang, and when I answered it there was John, dressed in full Braves uniform," Jeff recalls. "I'm talking hat, stirrups, glove, and all. I fell on the floor laughing. We played for a couple of hours, and when John left, I found myself praying that he would get stopped for speeding so he would

JULY

29

1994

A Great Day in Baseball

Michael Jordan hit his first home run, in his 354th at bat, playing left field for the Birmingham Barons, a Class AA team in the Chicago White Sox farm system.

have to explain to the policeman why he rides around in the middle of the night, [dressed like he's] ready to take the mound."

John's wily sense of humor is legendary with the Braves, but even more striking is his quiet, growing faith.

John was always the good kid on the block. He didn't get into trouble, smoke, drink, or chew tobacco, but he didn't become a Christian until after he began his professional baseball career.

How did John begin this journey that has led to baseball stardom and genuine faith in Christ?

John takes it all the way back to the minor leagues, where he played with Christian men who later became fellow Braves. They were Marty Clary and Jose Alvarez and Carlos Rico, who both pitched for the Braves in the 1980s. These men simply lived what they said they believed. It made a strong impression on John.

Baseball Quiz

My manager, Tommy Lasorda, gave me the nickname Bulldog. I'm not a hefty guy, but I know the art of pitching. I once pitched 59 straight innings of shutout ball (a record). I also sang the "Doxology" on *The Tonight Show with Johnny Carson* in 1988. Who am I?

Answer: Orel Hershiser

MAY 24 1994

A Great Day in Baseball

Seattle Mariner Ken Griffey Jr. smashes his 21st home run of the season to break Mickey Mantle's record for the most homers in the first two months of a season.

In 1989, when John made it to the show, first baseman Sid Bream and pitcher Greg McMichael became strong influences in his life. John regards them as "God's point men," who kept guiding him to Christ.

Because of these men, John attended baseball chapel and remained open to the truth. Over the years, the impact became greater and stronger until John eventually began speaking of his faith in Christ.

Bream says, "I get such pleasure in going out with John now and hearing him share his testimony, and seeing how he has gone from a man who spent his life trying to impress others and himself to a man who finds confidence, peace, and contentment through a relationship with Jesus Christ."

John's current teammates have seen the change. John has emerged as the Christian leader on the Braves. They know him as a person who once trusted in people and psychology but now trusts God about everything.

He explains, "I am no longer in bondage to the things of this world. My decision-making process has changed as my priorities have changed. My life has taken a turn of happiness and contentment because I no longer try to seek the approval of everyone else. The Lord is the one I am concerned about pleasing now, and as long as I know I have been successful in that, then I have been successful in life."

He cites a verse in Galatians that has guided him: "Galatians 1:10 says, 'Am I now trying to win the approval of men, or of God? Or am I trying to please men? If I were still trying to please men, I would not be a servant of Christ.'"

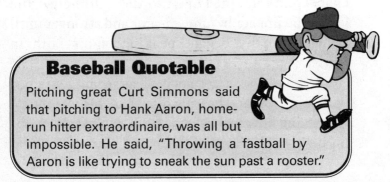

Baseball Quotable

Pitching great Curt Simmons said that pitching to Hank Aaron, home-run hitter extraordinaire, was all but impossible. He said, "Throwing a fastball by Aaron is like trying to sneak the sun past a rooster."

John concludes emphatically, "I am done trying to please men."

This turnaround has changed John's life. He notes, "I am now trying to raise my family in a God-honoring way, according to the principles God set forth in the Bible. I have a greater love for [my

Baseball Humor

For many players, base stealing is an obsession. With Hermann "Germany" Schaefer, it was an art form. In 1911 this clown prince of baseball was known as much for his on-base antics as his hitting. In one game, he was on first base, while his teammate Clyde Milan was on third. Hoping to draw the catcher's attention from home plate to second base—and to send Milan home—Schaefer sprinted for second. The catcher didn't throw, though, and Milan remained at third.

Piqued that the catcher didn't attempt to throw him out, Schaefer decided to pull one of his tricks. On the next pitch he ran back to first. He stole first! The catcher watched in amazement when, on the next play, Schaefer tried to steal second base for the second time that at-bat. This time, the catcher did try to throw Schaefer out. But Schaefer beat the throw—and in the process—Milan made it home.

Needless to say, such antics didn't remain standard operating procedure for clowns like Schaefer. The rules were changed to prevent anyone from stealing first base from the second-base location.

SEPTEMBER
22
1911

A Great Day in Baseball

Cy Young, baseball's winningest pitcher (playing for the Boston Braves) wins his 511th (and final) game against Pittsburgh, a record that may never be broken.

wife] Dyan, and I feel one of the most important things I can do for my children is to love their mom and show them that the things I say aren't just words, but are how I really live my life."

John attends a year-round Bible study in Atlanta. It includes former Green Bay Packer Mike McCoy, who co-directs the Braves' chapel program. Former major-league stars Brett Butler and Terry Pendleton, as well as several current players, also attend. Through the study, John believes he has come to know and believe the Bible in a way he never experienced before, applying it to life situations in his home and on the field. He likes praying and studying with men he once played against. All the competitiveness has been transformed into a common love for Christ.

John is now so teachable that at one point he was challenged to read the Book of Philippians each day for twenty-one days. Tim Cash, one of the co-founders of the Braves' chapel, advised John to look for ways Paul's letter tells Christians to serve others and have joy in spite of circumstances. John proved faithful, and his performance-driven self-image began to change. He soon felt a freedom in life and in pitching that he never had before. He was no longer playing for the crowd or even himself. He was playing strictly for God.

In recent years, John has built a close friendship with Jeff Foxworthy. The well-known comedian has begun his own adventure in Christ alongside John. Jeff noticed that John's quiet, cool spirit was rubbing

Baseball Quotable

Players often use the off-season to keep in shape. Steve Wilson, a lefty for the Dodgers, decided to prepare for the 1993 season by pitching in the basement of a sporting goods store in his hometown. Ron Perranoski, the Dodgers' pitching coach, heard about it and was pleased, but then he fired off this line: "That's not what I meant when I told him he should be throwing inside more."

off on him. Now, he, too, has learned not to rely too much on what others think.

Both men realize that their fame and fortune give them a great stump to speak from. John's attitude about the media and the constant barrage of questions he gets from fans is rooted in the Bible. "To whom much is given," he says, "much is required."

John remains the hard-driving pitcher he always was. But there is a difference. "I'm still going to go out and give it all I've got," he explains. "I just don't play for the records or the popularity anymore. I play for no one other than the Lord now, and when you play only for him, it really removes the pressure you once had. You can go out and have fun and work hard."

Baseball Quiz

Not many guys get to play with the same team their whole career, especially in recent trade-happy years. But I played with the Orioles from 1976–1988, and I was known as a pitcher with great control and a 1.63 ERA in postseason play. When I became a Christian, many said I would lose my edge, but I didn't. When I retired, I became an evangelist. Who am I?

Answer: Scott McGregor

Mini-Moment of Truth in Baseball History with Dave Dravecky

August 10, 1989. For most of us, it was just another day. For Dave Dravecky, a pitcher for the San Francisco Giants, it was a day that will live in his memory as his greatest baseball triumph. That day he returned to the major leagues after living through a pitcher's nightmare: cancer in the largest muscle of his left arm, his pitching arm.

It all started in 1987 as a little lump in his deltoid muscle. Dave thought at first it was a muscle spasm or perhaps a knot. When he consulted with his trainer, he decided it was nothing to worry about. By January 1988, though, the lump had grown.

Over the next year, Dave underwent surgery, losing much of the muscle in his left arm. He finally began a comeback, playing in several Class AAA games on his way to rejoining the Giants.

San Francisco prepared an incredible welcome for Dave's return, against the Reds in San Francisco. His story filled the news. The whole world seemed to be rooting for this comeback kid. The giant scoreboard in centerfield lit up in monstrous letters: "Welcome back, Dave!"

Dravecky took the mound. More than 55,000 fans roared. He was about to do something no baseball player had ever done. With only half a deltoid muscle in his pitching arm, Dave Dravecky meant to pitch in the majors, to throw sliders, curves, and fastballs at some of the best batters on earth. Undoubtedly, many people hoped he wouldn't have to hobble off the field, weak and undone. The crowd, though, gave him a standing ovation just for being there.

As Dave stood on the field near the mound, he prayed, "Thank you, Lord. Thank you for the privilege of doing this again. Thank you that you restored my arm so I could pitch. But most of all, thank you for what you've done for me. Thank you for saving me. Thank you for your love in Jesus Christ."

Then he stepped up to pitch.

The throw. High and outside. Ball one.

The crowd roared.

Second pitch. Fastball. High and inside. Luis Quinones fouled it off down the third-base line.

Another roar.

Third pitch. Backdoor slider. Low, outside corner. Strike two. Dave moved ahead in the pitch count.

Two more sliders missed the strike zone, however, and the count was 3–2.

Dave had to finish it; retire his first batter after a year-long comeback. That pitch, another backdoor slider, fooled Quinones as it hooked out of the strike zone as it crossed the plate. Quinones went after the ball, but got only a piece of it. A pop fly. One out.

The crowd shrieked. They were on their feet again. The adrenaline pumped through Dave Dravecky like Niagara Falls.

The next two batters went down in succession.

As Dave ran into the dugout, the crowd stood, cheered, and clapped again.

WELCOME BACK, DAVE!

It went that way through seven innings. The Giants scored several runs to make the game 4–0. Would Dave get a comeback shutout?

No. In the seventh, Dave began having control problems. No one noticed, but Dave knew it. He could easily get into trouble in the next inning.

In the eighth, Dave allowed the first batter to get a broken-bat single. He knew he could still lose the game. Soon, two men were on base, and Dave handed Quinones a pearl. He knocked it out of the park. The crowd was silent. Suddenly, San Francisco's early 4–0 lead was cut to 4–3.

It could end up a loss. But when Dave went into the dugout, the stadium gave him another standing ovation.

Dave didn't pitch the top of the ninth. Steve Bedrosian, the Giants' stopper, took the mound. Immediately, the crowd went wild. Another standing ovation. Terry Kennedy, Dave's friend and catcher, yelled at Dave, who was still sitting in the dugout, "Go on out there. It's your day. Take a bow."

Dave was embarrassed. But he finally went out.

As if that wasn't enough, the crowd wouldn't stop. It looked like a win for a man playing baseball after nearly a year of illness.

Dave bowed for fourteen standing ovations that day. In the end, he racked up a win, with Bedrosian saving the game for Dravecky and the Giants. Dave had come back. And with real fireworks!

In the locker room, Dave again shared his faith before the cameras and the world. "It's important for me to give credit where credit is due," he said. "I want to give praise and glory to Jesus Christ for allowing me the opportunity to come back and play again." He thanked his doctors, friends, therapists, and family, then answered many questions. It was one of the most inspiring, startling, and unlikely comebacks in baseball history.

3

SEAN CASEY:
A Good Guy at the Plate

Personal	Height: 6′ 4″ Weight: 225
	Spouse: Mandi
	Hometown: Upper St. Clair,
	     Pennsylvania
	Birth date: July 2, 1974,
	     Willingboro, New Jersey

Professional	Team: Cincinnati Reds Throws: Right Bats: Left Position: First Base
Records and Stats	Reached base seven times in a single major league game (May 19, 1999)—shares record Had a .544 slugging percentage in 1996 in Carolina League Named to 1999 National League All-Star Team

Photo by: Jonathan Daniel / Allsport

Career Batting Stats

Year	Team	G	AB	R	H	2B	3B	HR	RBI	TB	BB	SO	SB	CS	OBP	SLG	AVG
1997	Cle	6	10	1	2	0	0	0	1	2	1	2	0	0	.333	.200	.200
1998	Cin	96	302	44	82	21	1	7	52	126	43	45	1	1	.365	.417	.272
1999	Cin	151	594	103	197	42	3	25	99	320	61	88	0	2	.399	.539	.332
2000	Cin	133	480	69	151	33	2	20	85	248	52	80	1	0	.385	.517	.315
2001	Cin	145	533	69	165	40	0	13	89	244	43	63	3	1	.369	.458	.310
TOTALS		409	1468	229	460	102	6	56	260	940	200	278	5	4	.382	.490	.311

Major-league players who make it to first base when Sean Casey is manning the position are in for a conversation. For instance, Al Martin, playing for Pittsburgh, stood beside Sean after hitting a single. At the time, Pittsburgh had begun talking to San Diego about trading Martin, which they later did.

The first thing Sean said to his opponent was, "I've enjoyed watching you play. I hope everything works out for you. I couldn't imagine you wearing another uniform."

Sean chatted away while taking throws from the pitcher to keep Martin in check. Suddenly, Martin interrupted him. He said, "Excuse me, but I think I'll steal second base."

Not to be outdone, Sean replied, "If anyone can do it, you can!"

Martin talked to reporters after the game, quite amazed. "I've never had anyone talk to me like that [at first base]. The amazing thing about it is, he is sincere."

In another situation, Chicago Cubs Mark Grace took first base. Sean immediately began his chatter, telling the .300 hitter that he admired him—even to the point of asking for Grace's autograph after the game. Grace replied, "I should be getting yours. You can hit."

Sean replied, "You should know, you've been doing it for fourteen years."

Always a talkative, friendly guy, even as a kid, Sean has made a mark in pro baseball by being one of the nicest guys to grace the game. He's friendly.

JUNE 25 1968

A Great Day in Baseball

Bobby Bonds whacks a grand slam in his first major-league game for the San Francisco Giants.

He never forgets a face. Fans say that if you've ever talked to him and come back a year later, he remembers you and your name.

But the major leagues were almost lost to Sean after his trade from Cleveland to Cincinnati. Just hours before the opening of the 1998 season, Sean was blindsided when Damian Jackson hit him in the right eye with a pitch. Sean was laid up for days in the hospital, unable to see. Surgeons operated twice, putting five screws and a titanium plate around his eye. Sean didn't know if he would ever play baseball again. But his optimism didn't diminish in the least. He told his parents that he knew the Lord had plans for him. Whether it

Baseball Humor

The one event that helped baseball regain its honor after the strike of 1994 occurred in 1995, when Cal Ripken broke Lou Gehrig's Iron Man record of playing in 2,130 consecutive games. In April, before Ripken had broken the mark, Tom Goodwin of the Royals was having a bad day. First, Ripken robbed him of a hard-earned single by snagging the ball at shortstop and throwing him out. Next, the tough-playing Ripken tagged Goodwin out at second on an attempted steal.

Goodwin was incensed and later commented, "I wasn't too thrilled when he made that play or when he tagged me out. I was thinking, 'Why doesn't he take a day off?'"

was baseball or something else, it was all right. He knew he was in good hands.

Sometimes people compare Sean with Forrest Gump. Not because he's dumb, but because he's a great guy who enjoys life and lives it to the max. That's been his way ever since childhood.

Much of that childhood took place in Pennsylvania, in a little town called Upper St. Clair. There, Sean's father taught him to work hard and live by the Golden Rule. Sean often saw his dad praying for him and the family while he was growing up. That pattern had an effect. Before games, Sean will sneak out of the locker room and find a quiet place to read his Bible and pray.

It all goes back to a pair of parents who were committed Christians and transmitted that to their son. For instance, Sean learned early on about the honesty the Bible required. When he was thirteen, he and some friends stopped by a local store and secretly opened packs of baseball cards. They kept the ones they wanted. As they headed home, they were caught by security. They called the kids' parents, and Sean's dad drove down to pick him up.

Arriving home, Sean's dad took a walk to calm himself. When he returned, he gave Sean a dictionary and had him look up several words: greed, selfish, thief. Then his father noted that there are no shortcuts in life. You pay your dues, work hard, and maybe God will bless you with success. There is no other way.

Sean took it to heart. Today, his kindness and honesty are legendary. One night a young man named Shane Whiteman met Sean in the parking lot after a game. Whiteman saw Sean carrying a Bible, and they talked about faith, Jesus, and life. They became friends.

Several weeks later, Shane, upset over the death of his stepfather, found Sean and asked for help. The family couldn't afford to pay for the funeral.

Sean immediately opened his wallet and was about to give the boy everything he had. But Shane said no, all he wanted was for Sean to come to a local baseball card shop and sign autographs to raise the money. Sean obliged, the autographs were signed, and the bill was paid.

JUNE 23 1971 A Great Day in Baseball

Rick Wise of the Philadelphia Phillies did everything while playing the Cincinnati Reds — he pitched a no-hitter, smashed two pitches for home runs, and drove in three of the four runs scored. It ended 4–0, Phillies.

Why did Sean do it? As a publicity stunt? No. He just cares about people.

Sean is now a power hitter on the Reds, batting .332 in 1999 and .315 in 2000. His hitting prowess goes back to high school, where he excelled and hit over .400. He led his team to the Western Pennsylvania title in 1992. From there, he went to college at the University of Richmond. In 1995, Sean led Richmond to the NCAA Division I Tournament, batting .461 in the process.

Even with all those honors, Sean never lost his servant's heart. While at Richmond, Sean's older sister encouraged him to do volunteer work at a cerebral palsy center. While there, Sean befriended a little blind boy who had never spoken. Sean came back week after week, and by the end of his stint, the boy was speaking.

In 1999, when the Reds won 96 games and were expected to go all the way (but didn't), Sean finished with a .332 average, fourth in the league. He had 25 home runs, 99 RBIs, 42 doubles, and 3 triples.

The persistence Sean displays at the plate also helped him earn his most important title: husband. He met Mandi Kanka, a former college volleyball player, through his best friend one night. She wasn't interested in Sean and told him she didn't even like baseball. But Sean wasn't giving up on her. He knew a good thing when he saw one. He was persistent and is now married to Mandi. She says that persistence paid off, because if he hadn't been like that, they never would have ended up together.

Sean says the greatest commitment of his life is to Jesus Christ and his Word. Baseball is great, he says, but it's not number one in his mind. He tries to read the Bible every day. His favorite passage is Matthew 6:25–34, where Jesus talks about the problem of worry. Sean says, "There are so many issues and problems you can worry about every day, yet I've found that when I worry about them and try to take care of them myself, it doesn't work. When I turn to the Lord and lay everything at his feet, he takes care of me."

Sean Casey Q&A

Q: Who is your favorite baseball player?
A: Chicago Cubs catcher Joe Girardi.
Q: What are some of your hobbies?
A: Reading, working out, and golf. These are things my wife also enjoys, and part of what brought us together.
Q: If you weren't a baseball player, what would you be?
A: Probably a teacher, or I would work in my family's business, Casey Chemicals.

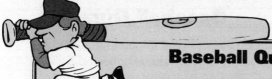

Baseball Quotable

Bryan Harvey, a pitcher with the California Angels almost ten years ago, was asked to tell his lifetime dream to a reporter in search of a great quote. Harvey, taking the reporter seriously, said, "Stop all the killing in the world." That was fine, but the reporter followed it up with a question about what Harvey's favorite hobbies were. He replied, "Hunting and fishing."

MAY 17 1970
A Great Day in Baseball

Hank Aaron, perhaps baseball's greatest slugger, got his 3,000th hit in a game against the San Francisco Giants. In his next at-bat, he smacked his 570th home run. Only three players in history have amassed more than 3,000 hits and 500 home runs: Willie Mays, Eddie Murray, and Aaron.

Baseball Quiz

Among players who began their careers after 1975, only two have collected 3,250 hits. Eddie Murray is one. I am the other. Also, at one point, I made a serious run at Joe DiMaggio's 56-game hitting streak. Who am I?

Answer: Paul Molitor (a committed believer)—3,319 hits, 234 home runs, and 504 stolen bases.

Sean knows well how easy it is to slip into that worry mindset. In a career in which you're only as good as your last game, your last at-bat, he has learned to keep his focus on God. He says, "There are a lot of temptations in the world, especially in pro sports. It seems like everyone is tugging you in different directions—some people for insincere reasons. That's why it's important for me to keep my focus on God and his will for my life."

You can be sure you'll be hearing a lot more from Sean Casey in the days ahead. As a first basemen. As an All-Star. And as a Christian.

That's a great combination for a baseball player.

Mini-Moment of Truth in Baseball History with Paul Molitor

Even though the hero shot of the 1993 World Series belonged to Joe Carter with his ninth-inning, series-winning home run in game 6, that edition of the fall classic was Paul Molitor's all the way. He was selected MVP after the final game, and it's no wonder. His amazing string of hits surprised everyone — except those close to him.

At thirty-seven, he was an older player, but that didn't mean he let up. In the third game, Toronto was six runs up. It was nearing one o'clock in the morning. Everyone was fatigued. Paul whacked a grounder to shortstop. For many players, a hit like this would result in being thrown out at first base. But Paul sprinted for first and made it. A clean infield single.

In the sixth game, the only homer wasn't Carter's. Paul blasted a 393-foot shot to move Toronto ahead 5–1. It was at that point, as he rounded second base, that he considered doing some theatrics. Maybe a little jig or a fist pump or something. But he caught his father's eyes in the stands, and that stopped him. He didn't want to make the Phillies feel too bad, so he just jogged along with no dramatics. It's that respect for the game that has earned him a reputation as a gentleman.

Molitor said after the World Series was won, "I definitely respect the game, and that's why I felt a somberness, a stillness, knowing how long I'd waited to feel that. It was everything I imagined. Days and weeks and months from now, I'm sure it will grow deeper in meaning. But right now I'm very peaceful with it. Yes, you get excited, and there's a rush of adrenaline. But there's something very peaceful about it."

When Carter smashed his series-winning home run, Paul wept on the field. He had wanted this World Series win — especially since being traded from the Brewers, who lost the world championship in 1982.

Paul was thrilled to join Toronto, the defending world champs. His new teammates knew Paul hungered for a World Series title. And they knew he'd done everything he could to help the Brewers in their unsuccessful run at the championship, how he'd blasted five hits in one game.

All the Blue Jays wanted to give Paul another shot. He was thirty-seven and quickly became regarded as an elder statesman and team leader. When the Series was won at the season's end, Joe Carter threw his arms around Paul's neck and said, "This is for you!"

Carter was expressing his appreciation for Paul's role in the victory. It was a role he played well. In game 6 of the Series, Paul stepped up to the plate in that fated ninth inning. Rickey Henderson was on base via a walk, and the second batter, Roberto Alomar, had flied out to left field. The Blue Jays were down by one run, and even if they lost this game, they still had one more to go. But wouldn't it be nice . . .

Paul thought that if he could hit a home run, the Blue Jays would win the game and the World Series — and he would go down in history. But immediately he pulled the thought back. He thought, *No, play the percentages. Keep the rally going.*

That's the perfect team player. He got the hit and kept the rally going until Joe Carter could deliver his huge smash.

Molitor is not one to go for fame and glory. He plays hard, and he plays smart. He gives his all, regardless of the score or time of season. He says, "Baseball can sell itself if it's played right. You play it the same way whether it's the playoffs, the World Series, or the preseason. I've had enough baseball taken away from me, so even grounding out is not that bad." (During the 1980s, he missed almost four hundred games due to injuries.)

Paul didn't do much grounding out in Toronto's World Series victory. He belted 12 hits, including a home run. He rang up a .500 batting average, with 10 runs scored and 24 total bases.

And his joy and gratefulness in victory moved his teammates. Pitcher Al Leiter noted, "We've had so much success here that people begin to think, *When are we going to play, and who are we going to beat?* Then Paul comes here after all he's been through, and you see how precious winning is."

4

ANDY PETTITTE:
Pitching Them into Fits

Personal	Height: 6′ 5″ Weight: 225 Spouse: Laura Kids: Josh, Jared, Lexy Hometown: Deer Park, Texas Birth date: June 15, 1972, Baton Rouge, Louisiana
Professional	Team: New York Yankees Throws: Left Bats: Left Position: Pitcher
Records and Stats	Drafted: Selected by the New York Yankees in the 22nd round of the 1990 free-agent draft Acquired: Signed by the New York Yankees as a free agent to a minor-league contract on May 25, 1991 Pitched more than 100 winning games for the Yankees.

Photo by: Jed Jacobsohn / Allsport

Career Pitching Stats

YEAR	TM	W	L	ERA	G	GS	CG	SHO	SV	IP	H	R	ER	HR	HBP	BB	SO
1995	NYY	12	9	4.17	31	26	3	0	0	175.0	183	86	81	15	1	63	114
1996	NYY	21	8	3.87	35	34	2	0	0	221.0	229	105	95	23	3	72	162
1997	NYY	18	7	2.88	35	35	4	1	0	240.1	233	86	77	7	3	65	166
1998	NYY	16	11	4.24	33	32	5	0	0	216.1	226	110	102	20	6	87	146
1999	NYY	14	11	4.70	31	31	0	0	0	191.2	216	105	100	20	3	89	121
2000	NYY	19	9	4.35	32	32	3	1	0	204.2	219	111	99	17	4	80	125
2001	NYY	15	10	3.99	31	31	2	0	0	200.2	224	103	89	14	6	41	164
TOTALS		115	65	3.99	228	221	19	2	0	1449.2	1530	706	643	116	26	497	998

Andy Pettitte is often summed up in one word: workhorse. Mr. Perfectionist, as he is sometimes known, pitches like a dream and has already amassed more than one hundred wins for the Yankees.

Every season he has started a minimum of 26 games. He regularly throws 105 pitches, putting a lot of stress on his left arm. His pitches often reach 93 mph. He has four pitches that regularly make batters scream: a cut fastball that makes righties swing and miss; a crafty changeup that keeps them guessing; a wicked curve; and a sinker that regularly produces ground-ball outs, thanks to the incredible Yankee defense.

Andy started in the majors on May 27, 1995. That year he went 12–9 with a 4.17 ERA. He almost won the Rookie of the Year prize but finished third in voting behind Marty Cordova (Minnesota) and Garrett Anderson (Anaheim).

Yet, for all his success, Andy doesn't consider baseball his top priority. In fact, when scouts came calling to watch the high school All-Star Showcase in Houston, Texas, Andy wasn't even present. He was considered the best pitcher in the region, but he had something else to attend that day—a trip with his church youth group!

A lot of people thought Andy was crazy. Miss a chance to impress professional baseball scouts? These were the people who sent you to the show. But Andy had other priorities. He had accepted Christ when he was eleven years old but really came afire when he settled into a youth group at Central Baptist Church in Deep Park, Texas. For him, the choice of choosing Christ over baseball was a no-brainer.

Baseball Humor

In a bizarre play, Keith Hernandez smacked a superhard grounder at San Francisco Giants rookie pitcher Terry Mulholland. The rookie snagged the ball, but it had been hit so hard that it lodged in his glove—wedged so tightly he couldn't free it. In desperation, he trotted toward first base and threw his glove—with the ball in it—to first baseman Bob Brenly. The umpire called Hernandez out. Then Mulholland and Brenly worked to release the ball.

JULY
11
1985

A Great Day in Baseball

Nolan Ryan of the Houston Astros fans Danny Heep of the New York Mets for his 4,000th strike-out. By the end of his career the Ryan Express recorded 5,714 strikeouts, still the all-time record. He led the league in strikeouts 11 times.

But that's not to say that baseball was unimportant. After a shining debut season, Andy went on to prove he was more than just another rookie sensation. His 1996 campaign was one to remember. He signed a one-year deal with the Yankees and ended up winning 21 games with a 3.87 ERA. As a result, he almost won the American League Cy Young Award, finishing second with Pat Hentgen of the Blue Jays.

That year, Andy became the first 20-game winner for the Yankees since Ron Guidry in 1985. He played in the World Series and even defeated Atlanta All-Star John Smoltz in game 6 of that fall classic.

Andy is also a winner off the field. He is a model father and husband. He is committed to rearing his kids in the Christian tradition, spending time with them each night before bed, reading them stories from the Bible. He prays with them and conducts regular family devotions.

Andy's baseball success continued into 1997, which was so good for him. He pitched in 35 games and won 18. He lost only 7 and posted a 2.88 ERA. He also completed his first career shutout, against the Toronto Blue Jays on July 5, 1997. He finished third in the Cy Young voting and earned several MVP votes, a rarity for pitchers, especially in the American League.

The year 1998 followed the same pattern. Andy pitched his way to a 16–11 record, with 146 strikeouts and 5 complete games. That was the year he began to be called Mr. Perfectionist.

But Andy doesn't let that moniker go to his head.

Baseball Quiz

I won 288 games, playing for six different teams (including the Yankees twice) from 1963 to 1989. I retired after having problems with my pitching arm — problems that led to a major operation. I then staged a comeback that many said was the comeback of the century. I became a committed Christian during that time. Who am I?

Answer: Tommy John, who played for the Indians, White Sox, Dodgers, Yankees, Angels, A's, then Yankees again.

"If you're a major-league pitcher, one thing is for certain," he says. "You're going to make mistakes. Believe me, it doesn't take much of a mistake for Ken Griffey to hit one out of the yard or for Mo Vaughn to smoke one off my forehead!

"Sometimes after I've had a bad inning, I'll think, *How can I be this bad? I must be the worst pitcher in this league.* But after the game, when I have had a chance to really think about things the way I should, I realize where my significance comes from: It's not about my winning percentage, innings pitched, strikeouts, or World Series rings. Don't get me wrong—those things are good. But I know what makes me significant is Jesus Christ and my relationship with Him. I place my trust in Him (and not me). It still inspires awe and wonder in me to think about these words: 'For God so loved the world that he gave his one and only Son, that whoever believes in him shall not perish but have eternal life' (John 3:16)."

Andy adds that his faith provides him perspective. "Pitching for the New York Yankees," he says, "could be the ultimate roller coaster ride if you let it be. This pitch is good. I'm happy. That pitch is bad. I stink. We win. I feel good. We lose. I'm depressed. The newspapers like me and think I'm good. I'm happy. Then I get knocked out in the fifth.... Well, you get the idea. Jesus Christ was perfect, and I'm not. And I'm OK with that.

"I'm grateful that God has helped me to avoid the big temptations that I have seen trip up some others. The big temptations are easy for me to avoid. There will be no drugs, no infidelity—and there will be lots of accountability. And I have always tried to discipline myself to avoid the more subtle temptations, like falling into a star mentality or lowering my standards of how I should treat people around me. I know God hates the sin of pride and arrogance. I have also seen how easy it can be for professional athletes to think they are entitled to superstar treatment. I know I don't want to go there—it could be a deep hole that's hard to climb out of."

As for the future, including baseball and beyond?

Baseball Quiz

The 30–30 Club is for the elite athletes who hit 30 home runs and steal 30 bases in a season. More than 20 players are in the club, but I'm the only one who did it as a switch hitter. In 1991 I hit 38 homers, stole 30 bases, drove in 117 runs, and made 30 errors. I also posted 30–30 seasons in 1987 and 1989. I spent most of my career with the Mets but put in stints with the Tigers, Rockies, and Cubs. One more thing: I love the Lord and have tried to serve him well on and off the field. Who am I?

Answer: Howard Johnson

"I know God is good," he says, "and that He has a plan. Here's my game plan: to give my life to Jesus Christ (I did that several years ago), to be a faithful and loving child of God, and to do my best as a professional athlete and husband and father. I will always try to stay close to God. And if we happen to win the World Series again, well, that would be just fine too."

Andy has found that his faith has served him well in good times and bad. He got off to a rocky start in 1999. Midway through the season, he had won only 5 games, while losing 7. And his ERA had ballooned to 5.39. Some fickle baseball followers clamored for Andy to be traded, but Yankees manager Joe Torre believed in him and kept him in a Yankee uniform.

Andy pitched better in the second half of the season, going 7–3 with a 2.95 ERA. He finished the season 14–11 with a 4.70 ERA, with 121 strikeouts. In the postseason, he pitched the Yankees to a 9–2 victory over the Boston Red Sox in game 4 of the American League championship series. Yankee owner George Steinbrenner, who advised Andy to "improve" earlier in the season, congratulated his pitcher personally—and rewarded him with a three-year, $24-million deal, one of the most lucrative contracts in baseball at the time.

Andy proved he was worth the money. He came roaring back in 2000 to post another great season.

Baseball Quiz

I led in the majors in strikeouts and wins for many of the seasons I pitched. I hurled seven no-hitters but never won a Cy Young Award or pitched in a World Series. I was an eight-time league leader in walks allowed. In fact, I'm the all-time leader in giving up bases on balls—more than 900 walks ahead of the second-place pitcher. Jerry Jenkins, co-author of the best-selling Left Behind series, wrote my biography. I owe my success to strong Christian values, a blazing fastball, and a hard work ethic. Who am I?

Answer: Nolan Ryan

He began the Y2K campaign with an 81–47 career record and an ERA of 3.95. During Andy's first five seasons, only Greg Maddux, Pedro Martinez, and Mike Mussina posted better records.

In 2000 Andy went 19–9 with a 4.35 ERA, striking out 125. From July 25 to August 24 he pitched in and won 7 straight games. A September 24 victory over the Tigers was especially memorable for Andy—it was his 100th career win.

And for the second time in his young career, Andy's Yankees made it to the World Series. In game 1, he pitched 6 and 2/3 innings. He gave up only three runs but ended up with a no-decision. He pitched again in game 5, with similar results.

But Andy didn't let the disappointment get to him. His head is screwed on right. He knows that

God has blessed him tremendously as a big-league pitcher, but he also knows that God is ultimately in charge of his career and his life. He's willing to take what comes and praise the Lord all the way.

He says, "If God took baseball away today, I don't know exactly what I'd do, but I know one thing—I'd be perfectly content, and I can honestly say that from the bottom of my heart. I've got a wife that loves me and that I love to death. I've got three kids. I'd be ready to shut it down right now and watch them grow up if I had to.... I feel that

Baseball Humor

In a 1979 game between the Cubs and the Mets, Bruce Boisclair whacked a low liner to Larry Biittner, the Cubs' right fielder. Biittner dove for the ball but was able only to knock it down. As he jumped to his feet, he lost his cap. Biittner wheeled around looking for the ball, which he was sure must be nearby. Meanwhile, noting the fielder's confusion, Boisclair dashed for second base, then headed for third. Biittner stomped around, searching for the ball as the fans roared with laughter, having seen where the ball went. It was under his hat.

When Biittner realized what had happened, he retrieved the ball from under his hat and whipped it to third base—in time for the third baseman to tag Boisclair out.

everything that's done in my life, God has planned. So if I happened to blow my arm out or whatever, I'd know that he was doing things for a certain reason, and I really think I could live with that."

Whatever happens next for Andy, no one can be sure. But one thing is certain: He'll be consistent, and he'll keep his eyes on God. And that will make him a winner, no matter what.

AUGUST 7 1952 — A Great Day in Baseball

Forty-six-year-old Satchel Paige, playing for the St. Louis Browns, becomes the oldest pitcher to throw a complete-game shutout, blanking the Detroit Tigers 1–0.

Mini-Moment of Truth in Baseball History with Gary Carter

Probably every kid has played the scene in his mind. It's the bottom of the ninth in the World Series. Two outs. Two men on. Behind by two runs. And you come to the plate. A home run will win it.

Or a hit will keep the rally going.

Anything — just connect with the ball and drive it somewhere where somebody isn't.

It doesn't happen in many games. But it happened in the sixth game of the World Series, 1986. Boston Red Sox versus New York Mets. The Mets were behind in the Series, three games to two. It was the tenth inning, with the Sox ahead, 5–3. Two outs. No one on. Two strikes. One more out and the game is over; the Series is over. Moreover, a home run won't win the game. It'll only tie. That would be good. But a hit — any hit — will put a man on base and bring the potential game-winning run to the plate. And then a double or deep single could bring about a victory.

To set the stage, here's a game recap, through the tenth inning.

The Red Sox and Mets scored one run each in the first two innings. Then nothing for two innings. After the fourth inning, the game was tied 2–2. In the seventh, the Red Sox scored another run. In the eighth, the Mets tied it again, on a hard line drive by Gary Carter — a key RBI for the Mets All-Star catcher. It was looking like Gary might end up with the MVP award.

At the end of the ninth it was 3–3. The game would go into extra innings, with a World Series championship at stake.

In the tenth, the Sox caught fire. Dave Henderson, their center fielder, led off with a home run. Mets' pitcher Rick Aguilera struck out the next two batters, but then Wade Boggs connected for a double. That brought Marty Barrett, who was hitting close to .500 for the Series, to the plate. He smacked a line drive into center for a base hit; Boggs scored. It was 5–3. It looked like the Series was over.

Bottom of the tenth. The Mets had to do something. The first two batters flew out to right and center. Gary Carter came to the plate, as his team's last hope, with the World Series at stake. Gary recalls, "I felt a presence in me, or perhaps beside me, a calming certainty that I wasn't alone. I was not, so help me, going to make the last out of the World Series. I felt certain of that. It would have been unacceptable, impossible. I would have lived with it all winter, and probably beyond. It might have stalked me for the rest of my career."

Indeed, Gary was in a pressure-cooker situation. Calvin Schiraldi, the Red Sox's ace closer, was pitching. He fired a fastball; Gary fouled it back. Then he threw another fastball right under Gary's chin. Ball. 1–1.

Next pitch, another ball. Outside. Gary was ahead of him 2–1.

It was all fastballs, and the next one was no different. Only this time, Gary drove it into left field.

A single — the most-needed hit of Gary Carter's life. He had kept the Mets alive.

The Mets went on to win that game, then the Series. As Gary Carter proved, sometimes your most important hit isn't a home run — or even a double or triple. Just a little single. But it can take you places you've never been.

5

JAY BELL:
Not Doing It Alone

Personal	Height: 6' 0" Weight: 184 Spouse: Laura Kids: Brianna, Brantley, and Brock Hometown: Phoenix, Arizona Birth date: December 11, 1965, Elgin AFB, Florida School: Tate High School in Gonzalez, Florida
Professional	Team: Arizona Diamondbacks Throws: Right Bats: Right Positions: Second base, shortstop
Records and Stats	*The Sporting News* named Jay as its NL All-Star shortstop in 1993. NL Gold Glove at shortstop (1993) *The Sporting News* named Jay shortstop on the NL Silver Slugger team (1993). All-time records with Arizona Diamondbacks for most runs (211) and home runs (58) 1997: Kansas City Royals Player of the Year 1999: National League All-Star Game starter

Photo by: Ezra Shaw / Allsport

Career Batting Stats

YEAR	TM	G	AB	R	H	HR	RBI	BB	SO	SB	CS	OBP	SLG	AVG
1986	Cle	5	14	3	5	1	4	2	3	0	0	.438	.714	.357
1987	Cle	38	125	14	27	2	13	8	31	2	0	.269	.352	.216
1988	Cle	73	211	23	46	2	21	21	53	4	2	.289	.280	.218
1989	Pit	78	271	33	70	2	27	19	47	5	3	.307	.351	.258
1990	Pit	159	583	93	148	7	52	65	109	10	6	.329	.362	.254
1991	Pit	157	608	96	164	16	67	52	99	10	6	.330	.428	.270
1992	Pit	159	632	87	167	9	55	55	103	7	5	.326	.383	.264
1993	Pit	154	604	102	187	9	51	77	122	16	10	.392	.437	.310
1994	Pit	110	424	68	117	9	45	49	82	2	0	.353	.441	.276
1995	Pit	138	530	79	139	13	55	55	110	2	5	.336	.404	.262
1996	Pit	151	527	65	132	13	71	54	108	6	4	.323	.391	.250
1997	KC	153	573	89	167	21	92	71	101	10	6	.368	.461	.291
1998	Ari	155	549	79	138	20	67	81	129	3	5	.353	.432	.251
1999	Ari	151	589	132	170	38	112	82	132	7	4	.374	.557	.289
2000	Ari	149	565	87	151	18	68	70	88	7	3	.348	.437	.267
2001	Ari	129	428	59	106	13	46	65	79	0	1	.349	.400	.248
TOTALS		1959	7233	1109	1934	193	846	826	1396	91	60	.344	.420	.267

The year is 1986. Formidable Bert Blyleven is on the mound, pitching to newcomer Jay Bell. It's Bell's first at-bat in the big leagues.

Blyleven's studying the plate. *This kid should be easy,* he must think. *Should be able to blow a fastball by him.*

The windup.

The pitch.

It's looking good.

Bell swings. Connects. Hey, that ball is soaring.

It's out of here! A home run for Jay Bell, in his first big-league at-bat, on his first pitch. And off of Bert Blyleven!

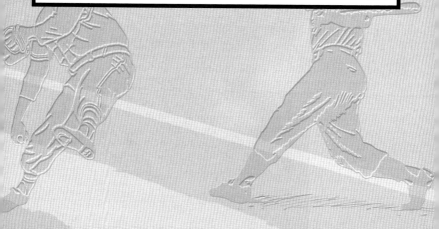

Andy Pettitte #46 of the New York Yankees delivers a pitch against the Seattle Mariners during game one of the American League Championship Series playoffs at SafeCo Field in Seattle, Washington.

Photo by: Jed Jacobsohn / Allsport

Paul Molitor of the Toronto Blue Jays connects with a pitch against the Philadelphia Phillies during game 5 of the 1993 World Series.

Photo by: Rick Stewart / Allsport

First baseman Joe Carter of the Toronto Blue Jays celebrates after a home run in the ninth inning during the World Series against the Philadelphia Phillies at the Toronto Sky Dome in Toronto, Canada.

Photo by: Rick Stewart / Allsport

Sean Casey #21 of the Cincinnati Reds walks on the field during the game against the Chicago Cubs at Wrigley Field in Chicago, Illinois.

Photo by:

Jonathan Daniel / Allsport

Mike Sweeney #29 of the Kansas City Royals smiles and looks on from the field during the game against the Anaheim Angels at Edison Field in Anaheim, California.

Photo by: Jeff Gross / Allsport

Jay Bell #33 of the Arizona Diamondbacks catches Mark Grudzielanek attempting to steal during their game at Dodger Stadium in Los Angeles, California.

Photo by: Jeff Gross / Allsport

John Olerud of the Seattle Mariners, left, is high-fived by Edgar Martinez after he hit a three run homer against the San Diego Padres at Safeco Field in Seattle, Washington.

Photo by: Otto Greule / Allsport

Tommy Lasorda, manager of the Los Angeles Dodgers, and Orel Hershiser, pitcher for the Dodgers, hoist the Major League Baseball championship trophy during their 1998 championship celebration.

Photo by: David Taylor / Allsport

Closing pitcher John Smoltz #29 of the Atlanta Braves throws against the Houston Astros in the ninth inning during Game 2 of their National League Division Series at Enron Field in Houston, Texas.

Photo by: Brian Bahr / Allsport

Catcher Gary Carter of the New York Mets celebrates after the Mets 8-5 win over the Boston Red Sox in game 7 of the World Series at Shea Stadium in Flushing, New York.

Photo by: T. G. Higgins / Allsport

Tim Salmon #15 of the Anaheim Angels rounds the bases during the game against the Kansas City Royals at Edison Field in Anaheim, California.

Photo by: Danny Moloshok / Allsport

A candid portrait of San Francisco Giants pitcher Dave Dravecky during a game at Candlestick Park.

Photo by: Jonathan Ferrey / Allsport

Yes, it really happened. Jay Bell walloped his first-ever big league pitch into the bleachers.

That's amazing. But it turns out that Jay had a little help.

Jay had come up from the minors to join the Minnesota Twins in the last five games of the previous season. Mike Hargrove, his minor-league manager, talked to Jay as they drove up from St. Petersburg, Florida, to the Tampa airport. He knew Blyleven was pitching and was renowned for his curveball. Hargrove said that Jay probably couldn't hit Blyleven's curveball so he might as well swing at the first pitch, which would be a fastball.

Jay recalls, "Bert had a no-hitter through the first two innings and retired the first two guys in the third. I went up there looking for a fastball on the first pitch, and I connected. After hitting that home run, I don't remember touching any of the bases. I remember dreaming about making it to the bigs and hitting a home run in my first at-bat. It was really a unique experience."

Jay has turned that promising beginning into a long, fruitful career. In 1999, he signed a five-year, $34-million deal with the Arizona Diamondbacks. Many critics questioned the wisdom of that deal, but Jay had a banner 1999, hitting 38 home runs. At one point he was the number two home run hitter, behind Sammy Sosa and ahead of Mark McGwire.

He also tallied 112 RBIs and scored 132 runs, as he sparked the D-backs to the best record in the NL West. In one game, he hit a grand slam that earned $1 million for a fan who correctly predicted the hit. Jay cites this gift as one of his career highlights.

In short, Jay has proven what the Diamondbacks already knew. He is a solid citizen, committed Christian, and levelheaded team leader. And he's a talented player, offensively and defensively. He won a Gold Glove as a shortstop in 1993. And he has hit consistently in the high .200s for more than ten seasons.

For example, Jay followed his breakout 1999 season with a respectable year of 2000. He hit .267, with 18 homers and 68 RBIs.

Jay became a Christian at the age of eleven, but he didn't become wholly committed to Christ until he got married. After he and Laura wed, they both knew they wanted to make a stronger commitment to the Lord. They made that promise, and since

Baseball Quiz

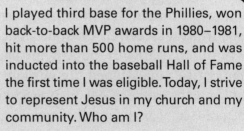

I played third base for the Phillies, won back-to-back MVP awards in 1980–1981, hit more than 500 home runs, and was inducted into the baseball Hall of Fame the first time I was eligible. Today, I strive to represent Jesus in my church and my community. Who am I?

Answer: Mike Schmidt

then Jay says his walk with Christ has been not only better but also more enjoyable.

Jay's faith has played a major role in his baseball career. He says 1996 was a big turning point: "[That] was the main time my faith came into play, as far as the baseball world goes. I was having a terrible year, hitting about .220 in mid-August, and I was frustrated. Baseball was not enjoyable, and I realized I was focusing on myself way too much. One day in Pittsburgh I grounded out and came back and looked at myself in the mirror and said, 'I can't do this alone.' I gave it over to God that day.

"It wasn't so much giving the game over, but taking the focus off me and placing it on others. It was about enjoying the success of others even though I was struggling. That's been a huge thing for me since 1996."

Jay says this new approach has made a difference over the past few years.

"Nineteen ninety-eight wasn't a spectacular year for me," he explains, "but I enjoyed it more than I would have otherwise, because the focus wasn't on me. The focus was on guys like Travis Lee, Andy Fox, and Dave Dellucci. It made it enjoyable for me to come to the park to see them have success.

"I think that's the key, not only to life in baseball, but to our walk with Jesus. Take your focus off yourself, put it onto him and others, and things tend to go a little bit smoother."

Q and A with Jay Bell

Q: Who was your hero when you were a kid?

A: Steve Garvey.

Q: Who influenced you the most, and why?

A: My dad was probably my biggest influence. He was my hero growing up. He taught me discipline and respect.

Q: What's the best advice you've ever received?

A: There's a ton of advice I've gotten over the years. Probably the best advice is to never give up.

Q: What players would you love to watch?

A: All the greats. Certainly Lou Gehrig, Mickey Mantle, and Babe Ruth.

Q: What's your favorite movie?

A: *The Shawshank Redemption.*

Q: What's your favorite TV show?

A: *M*A*S*H.*

Q: Favorite ballparks?

A: Busch Stadium and Wrigley Field.

Q: Best time of your life?

A: I'd say the day I got married to my wife, Laura, was the best day of my life. I knew she was the girl I wanted to be with the next sixty to seventy years.

Q: Weirdest thing you ever saw in baseball?

A: A lot of weird things happen out there with that round baseball, and I've seen a lot. Probably the weirdest thing I've seen is the ball hit by Sandy

Alomar Jr. that bounced off Jose Canseco's head and over the fence for a home run.

Q: If you could change anything about baseball, what would it be?

A: I would eliminate the DH [designated hitter] rule. I love the National League style of baseball [in which pitchers have to bat rather than being replaced in the batting lineup by a hitting specialist].

Q: If you weren't a baseball player, what would you be?

A: An airline pilot.

Q: Toughest pitcher you've ever faced?

A: John Smoltz.

Q: What you will do after baseball?

A: I might end up staying in the game as a coach or a manager. I've thought about it the last fourteen or fifteen years. At one point early in my career I thought I might make a good manager someday.

Q: Most embarrassing moment?

A: It happened in 1992 or 1993, when I was with the Pirates, playing at Montreal. I had a terrible night. At the plate I struck out three times. Also, I fielded a slow roller and tripped over the pitcher's mound and fell flat on my face.

Q: Greatest game?

A: Probably my first game in 1986, when I was with Cleveland. On the first pitch in the big leagues, I hit a home run off Bert Blyleven.

OCTOBER
12
1948

A Great Day in Baseball

Casey Stengel is named manager of the New York Yankees. From 1949–1960 Casey will take the Yanks to seven World Series titles and coach such greats as Whitey Ford, Mickey Mantle, Roger Maris, and Yogi Berra.

Jay's decision to join his current team, the Diamondbacks, was a tough one. He consulted with many people in the process. Several things pushed him to Arizona. One was Buck Showalter, the manager. Jay had known Buck for twenty years because he had grown up in the same area as Jay's father. Jay had a lot of respect for Buck and knew he'd like playing for him.

The second reason was money—more than $30 million for five years.

A third reason was that Jay wanted to play for a team he felt would make it to the playoffs. When he asked his friend Al Martin about Diamondbacks' owner, Jerry Colangelo, Al said Colangelo was the best owner in professional sports. Not just baseball, all sports.

That impressed Jay, but a few doubts lingered.

He says, "As I was flying out to Arizona to sign the contract, I was very concerned that I had made the wrong decision. I wasn't sure that I wasn't doing it just for the money. My wife and I had gone through the right steps. We had sought godly counsel.

Baseball Humor

Ever heard of a clean double that turned into a double play? It happened. On August 15, 1926, Babe Herman (not Babe Ruth) was a rookie playing for the Brooklyn Dodgers. Babe whacked a wall-banging liner with the bases loaded. The lead runner, Hank DeBerry, scored easily, but the man who had been on second was the pitcher, Dazzy Vance. Perhaps because he was a pitcher and was not used to being on base, he got to third, but then slowed and stopped just past third, thinking he couldn't make it to home plate.

Meanwhile, speedster Chick Fewster, the man who had been on first, did what was expected and headed to third, not noticing that Vance had stalled.

At the same time, Babe, not known for his speed or base-running skills, decided to stretch his double into a triple. He tore down toward third, while Vance was making his way back to third — and Fewster was already there. Suddenly, there were three men on third base!

Babe and Fewster were ruled out, and Vance was allowed to remain on third, since those are the rules for such a situation. And Babe was credited with a double.

I decided to hit it straight on. In my first conversation with Jerry, I said, 'I understand you're a believer.' I used the Christian lingo and everything and found out very quickly that he is a sold-out follower of Jesus Christ."

That convinced Jay he was making the right decision.

Jay's favorite books of the Bible are Isaiah and Daniel in the Old Testament and Galatians in the New Testament. But Proverbs 3:5–7 is a guiding light for him at all times. He notes, "I would say that's the main one for me. I look at those verses and say, 'That's what being a believer is all about. That's what makes Christianity tough.' It's not so much the acceptance of Christ that's tough; that's the easy part! It's the following of Christ and trusting that

SEPTEMBER 2 1907

A Great Day in Baseball

Ty Cobb stole second, third, and home in the same game, a record. He was such a fierce player that many said he sharpened his cleats to scare off opposing defenders — they feared being cut as Cobb slid into base in a steal attempt.

he's going to give you the answers. That's difficult. If we can, in everything we do, acknowledge that he has the best plan for us rather than rely on ourselves, then things are going to run a lot smoother."

What does Jay think people will say about him when his career is finished? He jokes, "That he was slow and had no range. [laughter] I would hope people will say there was something different about me, that I exemplified what it means to be a Christian baseball player. I'm convinced that as a Christian player I owe it to God, who gave me the ability to play, to go out and work as hard or harder than the non-believing player. Even though I don't have the talent of a Griffey, a Ripken, Kevin Brown, or guys like that, I owe it to God to work to be as good or better than they are."

Baseball Quiz

Detroit traded me, an up-and-coming twenty-year-old pitcher who hadn't yet played in the big leagues, to the Atlanta Braves on August 12, 1987, for Doyle Alexander. Alexander, thirty-six years old, ended up winning nine games for the Tigers the rest of that season—and losing none. The pitcher for the Braves, though, went on to post seven seasons winning 14 or more games, including a 24-win season in 1996, in which I won the Cy Young Award. I am also a Christian who gives his testimony regularly to those who will listen. Who am I?

Answer: John Smoltz

Jay works hard at second base for the D-backs, even though it's not his preferred position. He wants to do what his manager asks; that's his commitment. At second, he doesn't see as much action as he did at shortstop. In fact, he's involved in about two hundred fewer plays per season. In his heart, shortstop is the greatest position on the baseball diamond.

Second base, however, is a lot of fun, so Jay doesn't complain. And, as he did at short, he calls plays and shifts the outfielders' positions, as directed by coaches in the dugout.

Beyond the diamond, Jay has strong interests, including work with Young Life, Fellowship of Christian Athletes, and the YMCA. He speaks frequently for these organizations and is always willing to speak to groups and encourage them to persevere as they work to fulfill their missions— just as Jay Bell does it on the field.

Mini-Moment of Truth in Baseball History with Orel Hershiser

In 1968 Don Drysdale, pitcher for the Los Angeles Dodgers and now a member of the Baseball Hall of Fame, threw five consecutive shutouts. He logged 58-2/3 straight innings without allowing a run.

In 1988 another Dodger named Orel Hershiser finished his season racing after that supposedly unreachable mark.

But by season's end, Orel had tallied 59 consecutive scoreless innings, including 5 straight shutouts and 1 ten-inning no-decision, a feat that will stand for years to come. Orel Hershiser had done it. Drysdale's record had been broken!

When Orel broke the record, he couldn't stop grinning. The Dodgers mobbed him on the mound. In his 59-inning streak, he had allowed only 30 hits, struck out 33 batters, and walked just 8. It was a performance for the ages.

Orel would go on to claim the MVP award in the National League championship series against the Mets. He would start three games, notching one victory and two no-decisions. His ERA was a stellar 1.46. And, one night, with a game hanging in the balance, he volunteered to serve as a relief pitcher. He mowed batters down to win the game! In fact, he began the playoffs just as he finished the regular season; he posted eight scoreless innings!

Then in the World Series against the Oakland Athletics, he would go 2–0 with a 1.00 ERA. He pitched two complete games, a rarity in baseball's modern era. His first World Series win was a shutout; in the second, Oakland scored only two runs. From the beginning of his streak and continuing through the playoffs, Orel pitched 101-2/3 innings, 96 of them scoreless. He compiled an ERA of 0.62.

Orel's record for the entire year was 23–8, with an ERA of 2.26. He won his last 11 starts, a Dodger record that still stands. The National League Cy Young Award was his, almost unanimously. *The Sporting News* named him Major League Player of the Year. *Sports Illustrated* gave him the Sportsman of the Year honor. And the Associated Press voted him Professional Athlete of the Year.

Orel Hershiser had left his mark on history.

But something else may be even more remarkable. Sometimes people ask Orel how he withstood the pressure of pitching in front of 50,000 fans — and even more in TV land. He says, "It's easy when you know in your heart that a baseball game doesn't mean that much. Yes, it means a lot, and you are supposed to do your best. And yes, you have a responsibility to use your talent. So do the best you can. But then forget about it!

"[Early in my career], after pitching a bad game, I would lie awake and replay every pitch and criticize myself unmercifully. Later, I learned to replay pitches, pull out the positive things, and use them to do better the next time."

Orel's advice for young players? "If you think you have talent to play baseball, never give up," he says. "I was never thought of as a pro prospect because I was considered to be too small. But I knew I had a good arm and always figured I would play in the big leagues one day."

Through it all, Orel maintained a stout and unashamed Christian testimony. He says, "I really believe if you are consistent in your Bible study and prayer life, others are going to recognize what you have and realize it's something they want."

One hallmark of Orel's career was his habit of singing to himself in the dugout or even on the mound. The night after the World Series, Orel made an appearance on *The Tonight Show* with Johnny Carson. Johnny asked Orel about the singing.

"Do you just hum, or what? Do you sing?" Johnny asked.

"I sing," Orel answered.

The audience began clapping and cheering, and Orel realized what they wanted. He exclaimed, "I'm not gonna sing!"

Johnny said, "Yes, you are! Oh, yes, you are!"

There was no way he could avoid it. He had to sing. So he said, "Well, the one I can remember singing the most was just a praise hymn."

Suddenly, the audience went dead quiet.

"Praise God from whom all blessings flow.
Praise Him all creatures here below.
Praise Him above ye heavenly host.
Praise Father, Son, and Holy Ghost."

Johnny was visibly moved by Orel's song. In fact, he later replayed that segment on one of his best-of specials. It was a fitting end to an incredible season, a testimony for the ages. And maybe even God himself cheered!

6

MIKE SWEENEY:
A Royal Batter

Personal	Height: 6' 3" Weight: 225
	Single
	School: Ontario High School,
	  Ontario, California
	Hometown: Kansas City, Missouri
	Birth date: July 22, 1973, Orange,
	  California

Professional	Team: Kansas City Royals Bats: Right Throws: Right Positions: First baseman, designated hitter

Records and Stats	Led Carolina League with .548
	  slugging percentage in 1995
	Tied for AL lead in double plays by
	  a catcher in 1997 (13)
	16-game hitting streak (June 22-
	  July 7, 1999)
	25-game hitting streak (July 18-
	  August 13, 1999)
	1999—Kansas City Royals Player
	  of the Year
	AL single-season record (shared) for
	  most consecutive games with
	  one or more runs batted in—13
	  (June 23-July 4, 1999)

Photo by: Jeff Gross / Allsport

Career Batting Stats

YEAR	TM	G	AB	R	H	2B	3B	HR	RBI	TB	BB	SO	SB	CS	OBP	SLG	AVG
1995	KC	4	4	1	1	0	0	0	0	1	0	0	0	0	.250	.250	.250
1996	KC	50	165	23	46	10	0	4	24	68	18	21	1	2	.358	.412	.279
1997	KC	84	240	30	58	8	0	7	31	87	17	33	3	2	.306	.363	.242
1998	KC	92	282	32	73	18	0	8	35	115	24	38	2	3	.320	.408	.259
1999	KC	150	575	101	185	44	2	22	102	299	54	48	6	1	.387	.520	.322
2000	KC	159	618	105	206	30	0	29	144	323	71	67	8	3	.407	.523	.333
2001	KC	147	559	97	170	46	0	29	99	303	64	64	10	3	.374	.542	.304
TOTALS		686	2443	389	739	156	2	99	435	1196	248	271	30	14	.372	.490	.302

Mike Sweeney has enjoyed many great moments in sports—just look at his 2000 season stats, for example. He recorded 144 RBIs, a Kansas City Royals record. He batted .333, with 29 home runs. He was named to the American League All-Star team and was a real team leader.

But Mike doesn't consider year 2000 his greatest time in baseball. No, he reveals, "When I was twelve years old, I played on a Little League team. My brother was nine, and he was on the team too. We went undefeated that year. We won the district championship. What was so special was playing on the same team as my brother. That's the only time it's ever happened. He's my best friend in all the world, so it's really something. And my dad was the coach."

What was so special about that Little League championship game? Mike was pitcher that day, and he hurled a one-hitter.

"It was kind of a crazy game," Mike remembers, "because I hit five kids on the other team. And their coach was yelling at me and cussing me. I was practically in tears. I struck out fifteen kids and walked nine. But we still won 7–1. And my brother Richard got a hit late in the game. That was really exciting."

Mike's joy over his brother's performance reflects why he's often called the nicest guy in baseball. He says of his reputation, "I don't do it [be nice] for any particular reason, or to gain praise. That's just how God made me. I feel that if people

SEPTEMBER
21
1934

A Great Day in Baseball

Dizzy and Paul Dean of the St. Louis Cardinals whitewashed the Brooklyn Dodgers, twice. Dizzy pitched a shutout in the first game of a double-header; Paul racked up a no-hitter in the nightcap.

see that in me, it's just part of the fruit that is produced by the Spirit in my life. People have different spiritual gifts. I think one of my spiritual gifts is encouragement. I try to make people smile. It's not me that people see. When people say, 'Mike Sweeney is a really great person,' they may not realize that I am the person I am because I have Christ in my life. If I didn't have Christ in my life, I know I wouldn't be that way."

Part of Mike's niceness is that he doesn't push his faith on others. However, he makes his beliefs known. He's not shy about witnessing to his teammates, reporters, or anyone else. Frequently, he speaks at FCA Huddles in the Kansas City area. In the spring of 2001 he spoke at the Impact Rally with Youth Front in Kansas City, talking to about fifteen hundred young people and adults about his

Baseball Trivia

World Series shutouts are rare. There were only five during the 1990s. One pitcher, the New York Yankees Andy Pettitte, was responsible for two of the five. Pettitte pitched 8-1/3 innings of shutout ball against the Braves in game 5 of the 1996 World Series (which ended in a shutout), and 7-1/3 scoreless innings en route to a shutout of the San Diego Padres in game 4 of the 1998 World Series.

faith. He was cool and calm but also funny, a real storyteller. Afterwards, he signed autographs till he ran out of baseball cards to sign.

While Mike isn't shy about his faith, he also admits to not having a dynamic conversion story. "Many people ask me how long Christ has been a part of my life," he says. "I always tell people he's been in my life since I was young."

Mike doesn't remember a time when he *wasn't* a believer. He was reared in a Christian home in which his dynamic father led the family through his gentle walk with Christ. Mike says that his dad never "rammed anything" down their throats, but when the kids would mess up (there are eight in Mike's family), he would gently lead them into the truth. (Mike Sr. was an athletic leader too. He was a high-school All-American who went on to play professional baseball.)

A big moment in Mike's walk with Christ—one that set him squarely on the path of discipleship— came when he was a teenager. He says, "What really inspired me was when I was fifteen years old. I was on a retreat. I hung out with a youth minister in the back of the church, and we really talked about what it was like to have an intimate relationship with Christ. A minute-by-minute relationship, one where you always know he's there with you wherever you are. We were talking, and he just really hit me with it. You can talk to Jesus in the shower, you can sing to him in the shower. You can talk to him in the bathroom or [while] shaving, or anything. That day was one of the more joyful days of my life. It was a day that God's peace was in my heart."

Mike doesn't feel bad that he doesn't have a dramatic story, like being a former drug addict or alcoholic. But he recognizes God's grace has been with him for many years, and he doesn't play that down. He sees his success as a "God thing," not something he's done on his own.

And he's quick to point out that his squeaky-clean image doesn't mean he's without flaws. "It's not that I've been perfect by any means," he explains. "But I've always tried to live my life in a way that's pleasing to God." That has become the motto of his Christian walk: Be pleasing to God.

Playing for the Royals has been great for Mike. He likes the city, the people he's met, and the friends he's made. But it almost came to an end before the 1999 season.

There were rumors that Mike was about to be traded. The phone rang constantly, with friends and family asking if he'd gotten word of a deal. Mike didn't know how to answer. The newspapers were saying it wasn't a matter of if but when.

Mike still had not hit the big numbers he would rack up in 1999 and 2000, so there were many questions about his role with the Royals.

Mike says, "It was a time in my life when there was great uncertainty about my career. I didn't know where I was going to end up. My family and friends were calling and saying, 'Are you worried?' and I was saying, 'Yeah, I am worried. I'm comfortable in Kansas City. I have a house here.'"

Deciding to get things out in the open, Mike went to one of the coaches he'd become friends with. He asked point blank: "What are the chances of me staying here in Kansas City?"

The coach replied, "Mike, you have a zero percent chance of staying here."

"So," Mike recalls, "at that point it felt like the weight of the world was on my shoulders. My career seemed to be going downhill."

At that point, Mike contacted a realtor to find out about putting his house on the market. It was

Baseball Quotable

When St. Louis Cardinals left fielder Lou Brock made one of his spectacular dives at a line drive and came down with the ball in his mitt, Pirates manager Bill Virdon, stunned at Brock's skill, said, "He could never make that play again ... not even on instant replay."

Ash Wednesday. Mike decided to head for church. There, he knelt and had a long talk with God.

As he prayed, something amazing happened.

Mike recalls, "I was on my knees when I saw the vivid picture of my life—it was so detailed. It was a picture of a tandem bicycle. And I was on the front seat of the bike, trying to steer where I was going. And it struck me, 'That's why I feel all this pressure, because I'm trying to steer.' I cried my eyes out that evening. It was a time of brokenness, a time when I said, 'God, I cannot do this on my own. I realize I've been trying to do this baseball thing [myself] for years.'

"When I had given my life to Christ, I thought I gave him everything. But it was apparent that night that I was trying to do baseball all on my own. That night, my prayer was, 'Lord, I don't know where I'm going to go. I don't know what spring training has in

Baseball Quiz

Few big leaguers can say they were traded for two or more other players, but I was once traded for four. In 1984 I was traded by the Montreal Expos to the New York Mets for four veterans: Hubie Brooks, Herm Winningham, Mike Fitzgerald, and Floyd Youmans. I went on to lead the Mets to a World Series championship in 1986.

Answer: Gary Carter (a catcher and committed Christian)

store for me, but it's time for me to get on the back seat.' My commitment was that, come Easter Sunday, I was going to get on my knees and praise him no matter what. I told God, 'I realize that with you on the front seat of the tandem bicycle, you're going to steer me wherever you want to steer me, and I'm going to get on the backseat and pedal my heart out. I'm not going to get sidetracked looking to my left and to my right, I'm going to keep my eyes focused straight ahead on you.'"

In the weeks after Mike made that decision, friends and family continued the barrage of questions. But Mike had a new answer: "I'd say, 'You know, I'm not worried anymore.' They would say, 'Why, did they [the Royals] tell you something?'

Baseball Quotable

In 1993 Seattle Mariner Ken Griffey Jr. was so hot that at one point he hit home runs in eight consecutive games, tying the league record held by Dale Long and Don Mattingly. One of the homers happened during a game with the Cleveland Indians. Mike Hargrove, the Indians' manager, remarked, "He's so hot, he could hit a home run off Superman."

"I'd say, 'Yeah, they told me if I make the team out of spring training to pack my bags lightly because I'll probably be traded any day. So it's not anything *they* told *me*; it's that I now understand that wherever I am is where God wants me.'"

What faith!

God must have wanted Mike in Kansas City. He wasn't traded that year and ended up having a smashing season. He hit .322 with 22 homers, 44 doubles (tied for second in the league), and 102 RBIs. Up until that time, Mike had been the third catcher. However, Jeff King, a close Christian friend, retired, and Mike was moved to first base, which King had left open.

At first, Mike's fielding was criticized—he'd never really played the position before. But he improved quickly—on the field and at the plate. He began the season with a 10-game hitting streak and later racked up a 16-game streak from June 22 to July 7. He was so hot that fans and the media wondered where this guy had come from. Then, just two weeks later, he began a 25-game hitting streak, the third longest in the American League that year. It was also the third longest for the Royals, going back to the days of George Brett.

Mike says his faith has helped him improve his game. "Before, I was so wrapped up in myself, my pride, and my ego—and worried about my baseball career," he says. "Then I laid that down and said, 'Lord, give me your strength.'

"From that day, I've had the most peace and freedom about baseball I've ever had. In spring training (before the '99 season), for the first time in my life, I was able to play with peace and freedom, without worrying about getting traded. So every day I'd go out and bust my hump, and after each day I realized, 'I did the best I can in a way that would honor and give glory to God.' So why did I have a great year? The first reason is that I had a peace about my game in a way I never had before."

Mike's 2000 season was even better. He hit .333 and logged his best stats to date. He has become the cornerstone of a team that includes Jermaine Dye

OCTOBER 18 1977

A Great Day in Baseball

Earning the nickname Mr. October, Reggie Jackson cracked the first pitch in each of his three at-bats for home runs. The Yankees and Reggie won the World Series against the Los Angeles Dodgers.

(33 homers in 2000), Carlos Beltran, and Joe Randa. Mike keeps close friendships with all these guys, Christians or not. Jermaine Dye recently said, "The reason I like him so much is that he doesn't push people into getting involved with God. He leads by example. That's what a good leader is all about."

Mike likes to compare his faith with his sport when he explains his nice-guy but hard-hitting attitude.

He says, "My faith in Christ is kind of like the baseball team; if you're out there by yourself, it's going to be hard to win. If you're the only believer on the team, and you don't really have anybody to hang out with, or you hang out with a bunch of guys who will bring you down, it makes it tough. But for me, I've been blessed with some awesome

APRIL 17 1953
A Great Day in Baseball

Mickey Mantle smacks the longest home run in history, knocking the ball out of Griffith Stadium in Washington, D.C. The ball sails 565 feet and lands in someone's backyard. (Seven years later, he would break this record with a 643-foot wallop at Detroit's Tiger Stadium.)

friends. When I go on the road, I know I'm going to have several guys I can go grab dinner with, and maybe we can open the Bible and talk about what the Lord has put on our hearts at that time. That's so much better than going out to a bar or something like that."

What does Mike say to the young people he often speaks to?

"Our Creator intentionally made us with a void in our heart," he says. "Sometimes we try to fill that with our careers, money, automobiles—or some people go to drugs or alcohol. After a while you realize that those things don't fill that void. The only thing that fills the void—that gives you joy—is your relationship with Jesus Christ. People look at me and say, 'You know, Mike, you've got it all together—a great career, and you're getting paid a good amount of money.'

"But you know what? That doesn't fill the void in my life. That may bring temporary happiness, but joy is an eternal feeling that I have only because of Christ in my life. So do I want to experience temporary happiness, or do I want to experience eternal joy? I want to experience eternal joy, and the only way I'm going to do that is through my relationship with Jesus Christ and through growing in that relationship every day. That's what makes me complete."

Mike's deep faith has affected his team as well as players on opposing squads. He recalls one example of his influence, from a spring 2001 game against the Minnesota Twins.

Mike says, "There was a man on the other team who was a Christian. We knew each other a little; we both knew the other was a Christian. [At one point] he struck out, but the ball got by the catcher, and he made it to first base. As he stood there, he was cussin', saying words he shouldn't say. So I just tried to encourage him. I told him it was all right, not to worry about it, something like that.

"The next time up, he got a hit, and he was on first base. I was just watching things, but he said,

Baseball Quiz

I'm a pitcher who walked just 2.2 batters for every 9 innings pitched. I won 163 games, relying not only on my fastball but also on control and trickery to win. In 1980 I won 16 games for the Expos; I won 17 for the A's in 1990. My best year was 1991, playing for the Yankees. I won 16 games and was selected for the All-Star Game. In 1991 I pitched two one-hit shutouts, first against the Tigers and then against the Angels. That season, I walked just 29 batters in 208 innings. I am also an ardent Christian. Living for God and establishing family values are paramount in my life. Who am I?

Answer: Scott Sanderson

'Mike, come here.' He said, "I want to ask you to forgive me. I really felt convicted about those curse words when I was here last time.' I told him not to worry about it, but he said, 'No, it was wrong. Forgive me.' So I did. He was sincere, and it really hit me. He knew where my heart was in Christ, and he had the courage to come and talk to me. That was special."

What is Mike's final message to readers of this book? "If I could say one thing, it would be this: I got some great advice at not so young an age. I wish I'd had it much earlier. I was dating someone at the time. I didn't know God's will for my life. I talked

OCTOBER
15
1988

A Great Day in Baseball

Kirk Gibson of the Los Angeles Dodgers, having recently won the regular season MVP award, doesn't start the first game of the World Series because of a leg injury. But Dodger manager Tommy Lasorda sends him in to pinch-hit in the ninth inning. The wounded Gibson drills a pitch into the right-field bleachers to win the game. He pumps his fist in celebration as he rounds the bases.

to the team chaplain. He told me, 'Mike, imagine that you're running a race, and you're running toward Christ at the finish line. All you've got in your arms is what you want to bring to him. As you run toward him, you're leaving behind other things. But you're bringing things in your arms, too, like reading the Word and prayer and hanging out with other Christians. As you're running your race, look to the left and right and see who's running with you. Those are the people that you want to have intimate relationships with—whether it be a friend,

OCTOBER 13 1960 — A Great Day in Baseball

In the final game of the World Series — with the Yankees and Pirates tied 9–9 — Pittsburgh's Bill Mazeroski hits a home run in the bottom of the ninth. It was the only time the World Series was clinched with a home run — until Joe Carter did it again with a three-run homer on October 23, 1993, to win the World Series for the Toronto Blue Jays. The difference was that Mazeroski's homer came in a tied game, while Carter's occurred with his team behind by one run. Thus, both performances are World Series records.

someone you're dating, or someone else. So if you're running your race and the person you're dating isn't running with you, then you have to ask if that is who you want to run with.'

"For me that was great advice because that girl I was dating wasn't really going with me where I wanted to go. She wasn't running with me. So I knew it wasn't going to work.

"So the thing I'd say to young people is to picture yourself running in a race, with Christ at the finish line. You run as fast as you can toward him. Spend time in the Word. Spend time in prayer and with other believers. And then look to see who's running with you on your left and right. Stick with the ones who are running with you and shed the ones who aren't."

That's a great word for anyone who wants to play baseball, and also live for Christ.

Mini-Moment of Truth in Baseball History with Tim Salmon

Everyone in baseball dreams about it.
Few achieve it.
Tim Salmon did it.
But what is it?

An incredible, marvelous, super-fantastic rookie season in the majors.

During August of the 1993 season, Tim was making an impact in the minor leagues. So he was sent up to the majors on August 20. He played for the Angels the next night, August 21, 1992. He went 0–for–4.

A disappointment.

But the next day in Yankee Stadium, he collected his first hit, a single, against New York's Melido Perez.

The following day, he swatted his first home run, a solo whack, against Scott Sanderson, also of the Yanks. Clearly, he was getting used to the big leagues. Bright lights loomed ahead.

Then on September 2, the Angels were deadlocked in a tie game. It went down to the fifteenth inning. Two outs. Derek Lilliquist pitching. Salmon at the plate.

Crack!

The ball soared and spun into the bleachers. Tim Salmon had won the game for the Angels!

In 1992 Tim played in 25 games and hit .177. It wasn't glory. But it was a start.

And since he played only a portion of the 1992 season, 1993 would be his official rookie year. And what a year it was.

Consider some of the highlights:

- On April 28, Tim broke a tie game in the bottom of the ninth inning with a home run against New York Yankees' Jim Abbott.
- Twice he hit two home runs in the same game — July 27 at Oakland and August 18 against Detroit.
- He had three 4-RBI games that year — May 23 against Texas, July 27 versus Oakland, and September 15 against Seattle.

- He had a .980 fielding percentage, committing only seven errors in 354 chances.
- Among American League rookies, he led in a number of areas:

    Plate appearances — 610

    Games — 142

    Runs — 93

    Extra-base hits — 67

    Doubles — 35

    Home runs — 31

    RBIs — 95

    Walks — 82

    Sacrifice flies — 8

- Tim's last at bat of the season, against Seattle's Tim Leary, was a grand slam.
- He was the fourth player in club history to hit 30 or more home runs in one season.
- He was the nineteenth rookie in major-league history to crank out 30 or more home runs.

He was named American League Rookie of the Year, the first Angel to receive the honor.

It was a remarkable all-around season. And when it was done, come contract time, Tim negotiated the highest contract for a second-year player in the history of the game.

REFERENCES

Alexson, Bill. *Batting a Thousand* (Nashville: Thomas Nelson Publishers, 1990).

Carter, Gary and Hough, John. *A Dream Season* (NY: Harcourt Brace, 1997).

Cash, Barb. "Play Ball!" *Sports Spectrum*, October 1999.

Cash, Barb. "Cool, Calm and Collected," *Sports Spectrum*, October 1999.

Diaz, Gwen. "Priority Male," *Sports Spectrum*, May-June 2001.

"Guts and Glory," *Sport*, February 1994.

Lee, Victor. "Staying Power," *Sports Spectrum*, July-August 2000.

Littleton, Mark. *Baseball Sports Heroes* (Grand Rapids, MI: Zondervan, 1995).

Louderback, Jeff. "Mighty Nice Casey," *Sports Spectrum*, April 2000.

Marantz, Steve. "Shining Time," *Sporting News*, September 9, 1996.

Moriah, David. "Second Chances," *Sports Spectrum*, June 2000.

Palmeri, Allen. "Controlled Humor," *Sharing the Victory*, October 2000.

Smale, David. "Good Hit, Good Field, Good Guy," *Sharing the Victory*, April 2000.

Smale, David. "The Nicest Guy in Baseball," *Sharing the Victory*, April 2001.

Sorci, Rick. "Baseball Profile: Jay Bell," at http://www.findarticles.com/m0FCI/10_59/65131126/p1/article.jhtml.

Stewart, Wayne. *Baseball Oddities* (New York: Sterling Publishing, 1999).

Verocci, Tom. "The Complete Player," *Sports Illustrated*, November 1, 1993.

JEFF GORDON:
Driving Like the Wind

Personal	Height: 5'7" Weight: 150 Spouse: Brooke Birth date: August 4, 1971 Hobbies: water skiing, video games
Contact	Jeff Gordon National Fan Club P.O. Box 515 Williams, AZ 86046–0515 520–635–5333 Website: www.jeffgordon.com
NASCAR Facts	Car: #24, Chevy Sponsor: Du Pont Team: Hendrick Motorsports Crew Chief: Robbie Loomis

Photo by: Donald Miralle/Allsport

The year is 1997. The race, the Daytona 500. The announcer booms, "A million dollars, a mile away! Can anyone get by Jeff Gordon? He pulls them down the super stretch. Labonte looks inside, looks outside. No, it's Gordon in three!"

Back at Daytona, 1999. "Gordon is holding his line," the announcer says. "Earnhardt has to make the move. Nothing there down low. Gordon's car is glued to the bottom of the racetrack. Earnhardt can't do anything. Jeff Gordon wins the Daytona 500 for the second time!"

Daytona 1999 was one of Jeff Gordon's greatest races. Already one of the best NASCAR drivers of all time, the thirty-year-old speedster has many racing years and championships ahead of him. He will easily make the Hall of Fame. Being a championship driver is a long-time dream for Jeff. He started racing at age four—on his bicycle.

Jeff grew up a daredevil. He would try anything. His stepfather understood Jeff's need for speed. When young Jeff was four and a half years old, his stepfather walked into the house and said to the boy and his sister, "Come here. Look out the window."

Jeff ran to the window. His eyes sparkled as he saw two miniature racecars on a trailer. Jeff sprinted outside and checked over his new baby. Excited but terrified, he finally got into it and drove—like the wind.

Trivia Pit Stop

Jeff Gordon is the only driver to win the Southern 500 three years in a row (1995–1997).

Soon, Jeff was winning races. By age eight, he was racing on the quarter-midget circuit, blowing by his opponents like they were stalled in rush-hour traffic.

But Jeff almost didn't make it to age eight. When he was only six, he had a frightening accident. He recalls, "I got into a crash in a quarter-midget car. I hit the wall and flipped upside down. My foot was wedged between the gas pedal and the frame rail, and I thought I broke my ankle. I was screaming. I thought after that day, *I'm never going to get back in a racecar.*"

There was only one problem: Driving racecars was the only thing Jeff did well!

School? That was a bust. Other sports? He was too small. Musical instruments? Forget about it.

But racing? Man, could Jeff drive!

So he stuck with it. He celebrated his birthday every year at the racetrack. He won a national championship in 1979, at the age of eight, on his birthday weekend.

Then he won the national title again in 1981.

Jeff began to wonder what the next step was. He was getting older. He couldn't fit in a quarter-midget car anymore, let alone drive one. Besides, his stepfather's gift of years before was worn out.

So Jeff decided to try sprint cars, which pack 750 to 800 horsepower—on dirt tracks. Man, could they peel out! Soon, he was winning even more awards and honors.

Beyond the track, though, he was a shy boy who wondered if anyone noticed him.

"When I was at the racetrack, I felt comfortable," Jeff recalls. "But as soon as I left that racetrack, I was a very timid little boy who didn't excel at anything else."

He longed to run to the racetrack because that was where he did well. Nothing else seemed to work for him.

Jeff Gordon's teen years were tough. At times he ran with the wrong group of kids. But whether they were from the wrong crowd or the right crowd, few

NASCAR Starts Its Engines!

After World War II (1941–1945), car manufacturers began producing cars that were faster and sleeker than ever before. People wanted to race cars like these, vehicles similar to the ones they normally drove. They didn't want special racing cars like Formula 1 cars or the low-to-the-ground numbers you see in the Indianapolis 500. So, stock car racing was born. This brand of racing got its name because it featured cars normally kept in stock at car dealerships around the country.

In the late 1940s, various organizations were created to promote this new sport and keep it organized. These had acronyms like NCSCC, SCAR, NSCRA, USCRA, and NARL, with dozens of others in existence.

One man decided to bring order to this alphabet soup of confusion. Bill France Sr., known as Big Bill, gathered thirty-five important auto-racing people together in December 1947. Their goal: to create a national stock car racing body.

The group met for four days and came up with the name NASCAR—the National Association for Stock Car Auto Racing.

Trivia Pit Stop

Have you ever watched a Winston Cup race and wondered how many cars are competing? To make the race as safe as possible, only forty-three cars can be in the race. The first thirty-six cars and drivers are selected on the basis of fastest speeds in one qualifying round. (It used to be two qualifying rounds, but this changed for 2001.) Four more can get in as provisional racers if they are among the top twenty-five cars in the Winston Cup point standings (You can read about this point system in an upcoming Trivia Pit Stop.) Two more spots go to the top point-getters outside the top twenty-five. And the forty-third spot goes to the owner whose driver is the most recent Winston Cup champion and not already in the race.

of Jeff's friends at school knew about his racing life. He was often torn between his life on the track and his school life. At times he wanted to leave racing, to try to fit in with the other teens.

But during his fourteenth and fifteenth years, Jeff put the pedal to the metal in his racing life. Jeff's family moved from California to Indiana, home of the Indy 500. Here, racing opportunities abounded. He entered competitions around the

Midwest and began to realize how much he loved to race. And he learned to drive on asphalt. Until then, he had raced only on dirt. He loved the hard tracks. He didn't miss the mud at all. On asphalt, he discovered, you could really fly.

During his high school career, Jeff appeared on ESPN in various races in midget racecars. He recalls, "There was this live ESPN race, and it was the night before the Indianapolis 500—which is a big, big event. All the top drivers were there. We came out of the box, set a new pole record, and just zoomed away with the race. All of a sudden—bang!—we had something going! That got my name out to the general public."

After graduating from high school, Jeff decided to run against the big boys. In October 1990, he received invitations to three major races. He was just nineteen years old.

Trivia Pit Stop

When Dale Jarrett won his first Winston Cup race (1991) in Michigan, he nudged runner-up Davey Allison by only a few inches.

Pick up a copy today at your local bookstore!

Softcover 0-310-70292-5

We want to hear from you. Please send your comments about this book to us in care of the address below. Thank you.

Zonder**kidz**™

Grand Rapids, MI 49530
www.zonderkidz.com